DAVID ROSS

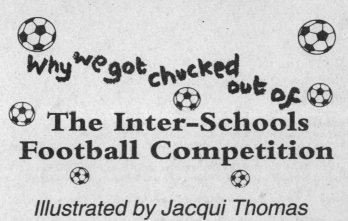

Why we got chucked out of The Inter-Schools Football Competition

Illustrated by Jacqui Thomas

PUFFIN BOOKS

For William

PUFFIN BOOKS

Published by the Penguin Group
Penguin Books Ltd, 27 Wrights Lane, London W8 5TZ, England
Penguin Books USA Inc., 375 Hudson Street, New York, New York 10014, USA
Penguin Books Australia Ltd, Ringwood, Victoria, Australia
Penguin Books Canada Ltd, 10 Alcorn Avenue, Toronto, Ontario, Canada M4V 3B2
Penguin Books (NZ) Ltd, 182–190 Wairau Road, Auckland 10, New Zealand

Penguin Books Ltd, Registered Offices: Harmondsworth, Middlesex, England

First published by Hamish Hamilton Ltd 1995
Published in Puffin Books 1996
10 9 8 7 6 5 4 3 2

Text copyright © David Ross, 1995
Illustrations copyright © Jacqui Thomas, 1995
All rights reserved

The moral right of the author has been asserted

Filmset in Baskerville

Made and printed in England by Clays Ltd, St Ives plc

1. The Goalkeeper (Ashton Jackson)

IT'S EASY FOR some people to criticise, isn't it? Blame the goalie. But our side only had to score more goals than the other lot did, and we'd have won. But we didn't score any goals at all. And I let in – well, I'll tell you later, after I've explained a bit more.

I have to admit, I wasn't feeling all that well. I don't even like playing football. It makes me nervous, with this big, heavy ball flying around. I might get hurt, and when I think about that, I get short of breath. When I get short of breath, I have to lie down. But you can't lie down in the goal mouth.

I didn't do any training for the match; there wasn't time. I didn't know until the day before that I was playing. I'm the reserve goalkeeper for the Skimpole Street School First Eleven (First and Only – there isn't another team). The regular keeper is Piano Legs Cooper. It was when he got chickenpox that they got on to me. Sarvindar Patel, he's the captain, said, "Jackson, you're on. You're the goalie tomorrow, against Stapleton Road."

"What?" I said. "You're kidding."

"I wish I was," said Patel. "We need you. Piano Legs is sick."

Piano Legs is never sick. He's the healthiest person I know. He's horribly healthy. That's why I've never kept goal before. I thought I was quite safe

being the reserve keeper, sort of in the
football team without having to play.
It started just because once, long ago,
they were playing football in the
playground. I wasn't playing; I was
having an argument with Margery
O'Neil about whether miles were
longer than kilometres. She thinks
they're not. All of a sudden I heard a
shout:

"Ashton, look out!"

I was standing right in front of the big window of the canteen. The ball came zooming down at me out of the sky. Without even thinking, I jumped up and caught it, with my eyes shut.

"Oof!" It knocked all the breath out of me, and I sat down very hard, still holding the ball. Everyone was very surprised, and Sarvindar, who was the one that kicked it up so high, was very pleased.

"It would have broken the window, for sure," he said. "You're a natural goalie, Jackson. Who'd have thought it, a wimp like you?"

"It was a fluke," said someone else.

"No, he's got fantastic reflexes. He could be an ace goalie."

"Well done, Wimpy," they all said. I didn't say I grabbed it just to stop it hitting me in the face. Ever since then,

I've been the reserve keeper for the
school team.

My mum didn't want me to play. She
said I was looking pale, and she took
my temperature, but it turned out to
be normal.

"I don't trust this thermometer,"
she said. "You don't look normal to
me. I'm going to buy another one. And
it's a nasty, raw-looking day. It won't
do your chest any good, standing in
goal for an hour and a half. Perhaps
you'd better stay at home."

I wish now I hadn't argued. But I
said, "Aw, Mum, I'll be all right. And
they haven't anyone else; I can't let the
team down."

The truth is, I was feeling rather
pleased to have been chosen. How
could I have known how awful it
would be?

In the end my mum gave my chest a
good rub with Super-Strong

Embrocation and made me wear a woolly winter vest, but she let me go.

I had to wear Piano Legs' kit. As he's about twice my weight, it didn't fit very well. I had to tie the shorts up with string, and if I lifted my feet off the ground too quickly, the boots fell off. That didn't exactly help.

I did try to keep goal properly in the match with Stapleton Road. But somehow, I never quite got to the ball. When I jumped, I didn't jump high enough, because I was too busy curling my toes into the boots and holding on to the shorts with one hand to stop the string slipping. When the ball came low, I never got there in time. Well, I don't like throwing myself on to hard, muddy ground. And sometimes it came really fast and I thought it might sting my hands. Once I did catch it, and was so surprised that I let it drop again, over the line.

"I don't believe it," said our captain.

"Well, keep them away," I said. "Go and score some goals up at the other end."

"Sixteen-nil," he said. "And it's not

even half-time yet."

When it all came to an end, the
score was twenty-two to nil. I don't
think I'll be asked to keep goal again.
Sarvindar Patel was quite rude.

"I'd sooner have your granny
keeping goal than you," he said
afterwards. "You never even got
dirty." He and the others had got
covered in mud. There was a long

skid-mark in the mud to one side of our goal where he had slid along, trying to get the ball away from the Stapleton Road striker. I don't know what my mum would say if she saw me like that.

"My hands were dirty," I said.

"Huh, from picking up the ball after they scored," said Patel.

Well, I don't care. I never asked to be the goalkeeper. The game I really like is tiddlywinks. I can beat anybody at that.

2. *The First Defender (Kevin Brown)*

I DIDN'T START the fight. It's always my brother who starts things.

"You take it," he shouts to me, when that big tall Stapleton Roader comes running up with the ball.

"No, you," I say back. "I'm marking the winger, can't you see?"

So the Stapleton Roader comes right through the middle, with Patel yelling, "Stop him, you idiots!" and slams the ball past Wimpy, who runs away in the other direction. The ref blows his whistle. Another goal to them.

"Why didn't you stop him, like I

told you to?" says Norman. He's my brother. My twin brother. Twenty minutes older, so he thinks he's the boss.

"He was yours," I say. "I had to mark that winger. If he'd passed the ball to him, we'd have been left wide open. You should have tackled."

"He was over on your side."

"No he wasn't."

"Yes he was."

"Anyway, you're not the skipper. I don't have to take orders from you."

"Well, if you'd done what I said, we might have saved that goal. You never listen, do you?"

"I don't need any orders from you."

"Both of you have to run more," says Patel. "You have to cover the centre as well as the wings."

Then it's kick-off again, and,

unbelievably, the ball gets into their half. It's hardly been there at all so far in the match. They've been all over us. Little Patel is up there, so are Jones, Gibson, Anderson, all the rest of them; everyone except Norman, me and Wimpy Jackson.

"Go on, Skimpole, score!" I shout.

But out comes the ball with the tall player again. He can run like anything, taking the ball with him as if it was part of his boot. I can hear Patel shouting. I've got to stop him. I will stop him. I can hear shouting but I'm not listening, I'm concentrating on taking the ball from the Stapleton Roader. Then suddenly there's a huge thump, and I'm knocked sideways and fall flat in the cold, muddy grass. My idiot brother has run right into me.

"You fool," I try to shout, but I

13

haven't enough breath. He's sitting on the ground too, glaring at me. He's got no puff either, but I can see his lips move, saying something nasty. A cry goes up from the Stapleton Road side. Lanky Long-legs has scored again. Poor Wimpy has picked up the ball and is holding it as if it's a bomb about to go off.

"He was mine," says my brother at last.

"No he wasn't. I was nearer."

"Didn't you hear me? I said to leave it."

I can feel my ribs aching where he collided with me.

."You pushed me."

"No, I didn't."

"You did. You put your fist right in my ribs."

"I was just trying to keep my balance."

"Liar."

"Don't call me a liar."

"Yah, liar."

"You're the liar."

"Rotten stinking liar. And you can't play football."

"That's another lie."

Okay, I suppose I did hit him first.

But he was asking for it. Even before
the football match. He'd been getting
on my nerves all morning. He took
three Weetabix out of the packet at
breakfast and only left two for me. And
he took most of the milk. And he eats
my peanut butter. Our mum started
getting the two kinds, crunchy for him
and smooth for me, because nasty
Norman says he doesn't like the
smooth kind. But today my jar was
nearly empty, and I know why. He's
decided he prefers the smooth sort
after all, and he's been sneaking it. He
thinks I don't know, but I do. I always
know what he's up to.

So I hit him, sort of, in the ribs, and
he hit me back, right on my sore ear.
He knew I had a sore ear, because I
told him. He just laughed, though.
Then later, he hits me on it. That's the

sort of brother I've got. I knocked him
over into the mud, but he pulled me
down with him, and I ended up
underneath. By the time the ref had
pulled us apart, we were covered in
mud. He had a black eye, and I had a
big lump on my lip. And my sore ear
was really aching. I accidentally sort of
caught the referee's leg with my boot
as he dragged us up, and he got really
wild.

"Off," he said. "Both of you. What do you think you are? Professionals?"

He was in a bad temper already, and that was before the dog came on the pitch and bit a hole in his shorts. So Skimpole Street was two men down, and it wasn't even half-time. Wimpy Jackson watched us going.

"What do I do now?" he wailed.

"Go home," said Norman.

3. The Captain
(Sarvindar Patel)

WHAT A NIGHTMARE! I'd sooner walk
the tightrope over a tank full of
piranha fish than go through that
again. My first time as captain, and we
lose the first game twenty-two to
nothing. In the first half. Not only
that, we get disqualified from the
competition. I'm not sure what was the
exact reason for us being thrown out.
Those stupid Browns didn't help. The
dog didn't help. Charlie Gibson's
injury probably didn't make much
difference. But Gary Sandford's
mother didn't help. And what

19

happened at half-time just put the lid on everything.

There had been problems from the very start.

The Head, Mr Watkins, got very excited. He's always excited about something. He comes from Wales and has bright red hair that sticks out over his ears. When he's really excited, his face gets very pink and his eyes look as if they're going to pop out.

"Patel, my boy, I'm making you captain of the First Eleven for the Inter-Schools Football Competition. You'll have the best turned-out team in the whole tournament," he said to me. "I've arranged with the Ghengis Khan Fast Food Takeaway to provide a new strip. Mr Abdullah was delighted to be asked. All he wants in return is for young Abdullah to be

included in the team. That's all right,
isn't it, Patel? You can fit him in
somewhere, can't you?"

"Aw, sir," I said. "Abdullah's
useless. He's too fat. He can't run. He
can't even see his feet – "

21

"Now, Patel, that's enough. We'll have no fat-ism in Skimpole Street School. Young Bayram Abdullah may have a weight problem, but that's no reason to leave him out of the football team. It may give him just the right sort of encouragement to try to slim down a bit."

"But, sir, he can't play football."

"Well, he's only one, isn't he? You have nine others in the side, plus yourself. And the new kit I've got for you should be a terrific boost for the team. It's worth having young Abdullah in it just for that. I've got a feeling that Skimpole Street will come out on top this time, for once. Now run along, and stop making difficulties. Think Positive, Patel!"

Mr Watkins doesn't like being contradicted. He always Thinks

Positive. I think that Thinking Positive just means agreeing with Mr Watkins.

It was all right in our training sessions. We had some good people in the team. Laurence Murphy is brilliant in midfield, and Piano Legs Cooper is a really good goalkeeper. And some of the others aren't too bad, including me. The Brown twins are okay when they aren't fighting. And even if he's only got one leg, old Mr Hitchin knows a lot about football. It's a pity his memory isn't what it was. He's our trainer, because we haven't had a PT teacher at Skimpole Street School since Mr Rumbold pulled the wallbars down on top of himself and broke his legs.

It wasn't his fault. He didn't know they had been unfixed so that the wall behind could be painted. Mr Watkins should have told him, but he was thinking about something else at the time, and forgot.

He did go to visit Mr Rumbold in hospital. We all signed a card for Mr Watkins to take along. But Mr Rumbold tried to throw a vase of flowers at him, which wasn't easy with two legs in plaster. He fell out of bed and broke his arm, which was just about the only thing that wasn't broken already.

So Mr Hitchin stepped into the gap
as trainer. He's Sandford's
grandfather. He was once considered
for Tranmere Rovers when he was
young, before he lost his leg. He can
still get up quite a speed along the
sidelines in his wheelchair. His special
combination tactic was going to be our
secret weapon.

"Get this right, and you're
unbeatable," he said to me. "Now, just
let me think. What was it? Was it
4-4-2? or 5-3-2?"

He took off his woolly hat and
scratched his bald head.

"Let's see, now. The centre-forward
takes the ball, and he passes it to his
left. No, his right. Or is it? Well, he
passes it and moves ahead to the
twenty-yard line. The inside right is
there to dummy, to make the defence

think he's going to take the ball from the centre-half. But instead the centre-forward moves to the right, no, the left, and the centre-half passes the ball to him. Now comes the clever bit. They all think he's going to try for goal, but he passes it to the winger – "

"Which winger, Mr Hitchin?"

"What? Oh, just let me think a minute, until I get it straightened out in my mind."

I never did quite get the hang of it.
And then, two days before, Murpho
fell off his bike and sprained his ankle.
And Piano Legs got chicken pox.
Things began to look a bit bad. I
admit it was a mistake to pick Wimpy
Jackson for goal. And I shouldn't have
paired the Browns in defence. I accept
responsibility for that. But I couldn't
help the dog, or Sandford's mother, or
what happened at half-time. You can't
blame the captain for absolutely
everything.

Then there was the new strip. It was
horrible. Sort of slithery nylon stuff
that crackled when you touched it. The
shirts were bright yellow. The shorts
were bright green.

"Hee hee, look, a bunch of
daffodils," said someone from
Stapleton Road when we came out on

27

the pitch, and they all laughed. The shirts had G-K Takeaway – Fastest Food in Town in big letters on the back, and Skimpole Street School in very little letters on the front. I was glad the pitch was so muddy, it meant that soon we were all just mud-coloured.

I could see they had done more training than we had. We hardly got to touch the ball. Their PT teacher was there, a little bony man with a frizzy beard, who kept on jumping up from his bench and shouting things like, "Well done, Hognose!" or "Tackle closer, Fruitbat!" Maybe they weren't called Hognose and Fruitbat, but it sounded like it.

Old Mr Hitchin got very cross, and ran his wheelchair over the other trainer's foot just as he was getting up.

He said it was an accident, though the man with the beard said it was common assault and he was going to sue for damages. After that he could only hop about on one leg when he wanted to shout something.

When the dog came on, we were all down at our end. They had just scored their sixteenth goal, and the Brown twins had been sent off for fighting each other.

I knew the dog as soon as I saw it. It was Pongo, the big Dalmatian from the Green Dragon pub. It's just down the road from my dad's office. He's a friendly dog usually. I don't know why he bit the referee. He likes chewing things like old boots, not people.

The ref was out by himself in mid-field, and Pongo went straight for him. He only bit a piece out of the referee's shorts, really, but Mr Davis was very angry. He went quite pale. He and Mr Micklewell, Pongo's owner, had a loud argument.

"He was just being friendly," said

Mr Micklewell. "He's a great big puppy really. He'd never have harmed you."

"He's a menace," shouted Mr Davis, keeping a hand over his bottom. "You set him on to me deliberately. I heard you say 'Go for him, boy.' I shall report it. You won't get away with this."

"I didn't," said Mr Micklewell. "I was just shouting to the lads. I said 'Go for it, boys' not 'Go for him, boy'. Pongo just got a bit excited.".

"I heard what I heard," said Mr Davis. "Intimidating the referee is a serious offence."

"I'm sorry," said Mr Micklewell. "It was an accident. Perhaps I can pay for a replacement pair of shorts."

"I shall make a full claim for

damages through the proper
channels," said Mr Davis. "Luckily I
brought a spare kit with me, or the
game would have to be abandoned."

He tried to twist round to look at his
bottom.

"I'm not sure he hasn't grazed the
flesh, you know."

"Let me have a look," said Mr Micklewell, but Mr Davis quickly turned round the other way.

"That won't be necessary," he said. "The game is temporarily suspended while I retire to the pavilion."

He started back to the pavilion, walking backwards away from us. Mr

Micklewell went with him, still trying to explain that Pongo was friendly. I wonder if the ref knew that Mr Micklewell was Kevin and Norman Brown's uncle. Probably not, or he'd have been even more sure it wasn't an accident. After a long time, Mr Davis came out in a fresh kit, and blew his whistle for the game to start again.

And then we did get a chance, at last. Through Bayram Abdullah, of all people. He was fouled, inside the penalty area. He was just wandering about up there, when I got a lucky break. One of their forwards slipped and fell when he was on the ball, and it bounced over to me. I gave it a mighty kick upfield and went tearing after it. There was no one there but Bayram. Luckily he wasn't offside. There were two Stapleton Roaders between him and the goal.

"Get it, Bayram," I shouted. "Boot it in."

But poor Bayram can't move too fast, on account of being so fat. He started to go for the ball, but one of the defenders got there first. Say what you like about Bayram, he's really keen.

He came wallowing along and tried to get the ball, but the other boy pushed him off. The ref saw it, and awarded a penalty.

Laurence Murphy normally takes the penalty shots. But he wasn't there.

Suddenly you find the whole world shrinks to twelve yards of muddy grass and a goal-mouth. The Stapleton Road keeper was in front of me. He hadn't had much to do, so far, but he looked as if he knew his job.

I knew exactly where I was going to put the ball. Smack in the top left-hand corner of the net. That goalie wouldn't even see it go past him. I can kick the ball really hard. I nearly broke the big canteen window at school once with a kick from right across the playing field, but luckily Wimpy Jackson stopped it.

Anyway, I gave this one everything I'd got. Maybe I was too keen. I overdid it. I hit the ball just too low. It flew up into the air, clearing the bar by inches, kept on climbing, and disappeared over the fence behind the goal posts. There was a sound of

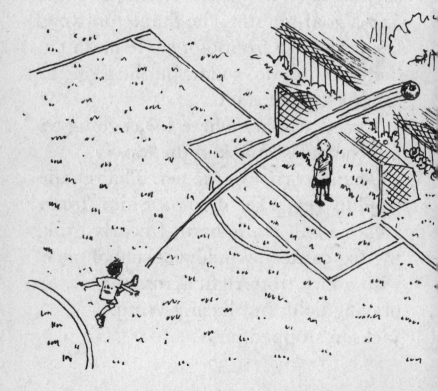

breaking glass. On the other side of the fence is the Willoughby Street allotments, with lots of little greenhouses.

I wanted to cry. But the captain can't cry.

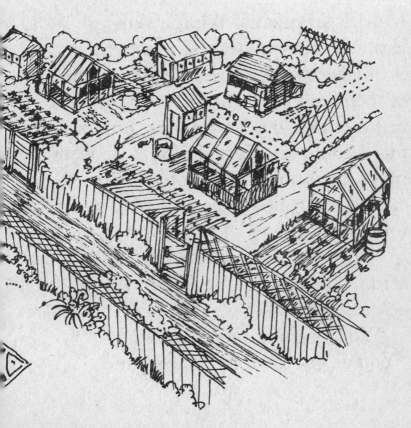

4. The Player as Artist (Charlie Gibson)

WHAT A SHAMBLES! What a shower!
Yes, my team-mates, Skimpole Street
School's so-called First Eleven. Some
of them know a little bit, but you can't
call them serious footballers, not like
me. I could see from the start we were
in for a drubbing. First of all Patel, the
captain, got the placing all wrong. I
told him.

"I'm ready to lead the attack," I
said. "You need some skill in the
centre."

"You're going back," he said.
"You've got the longest legs, and

we need a sweeper."

It's not that I want to be skipper myself. I could be, of course, but I'm basically a loner. There's an International player I model myself on, he's just my type – well, you'd only have to see me play to realise who I mean. We're so similar, it's amazing. I'm surprised that people don't seem to notice. It's a question of style. Brilliant, yes; good to watch, yes; temperamental, maybe, but with a right to be. When you're as good as that, you need things to be just right, and if they're not, then you owe it to yourself to complain.

Too many things that day weren't right for me. The weather for a start. Cold, windy, then it started to rain. I think I'll probably sign for an Italian club later, when I've turned professional. They have better weather there. Then to be stuck as a sweeper. No wonder I was seriously off form. Treating me as just another team player just isn't the way to get the best out of me. I need space to show my talent, out in front, leading the attack.

And the other side, Stapleton Road School, weren't the right sort of opposition. Don't get me wrong, I know that possession is the name of the game, but I'm not a physical player. Artistry is what I have – ball control, placing a lob just in the right spot, the well-timed header. But when these forwards just come crashing through, with their trainer howling at them to tackle, there's no chance. I don't know how many times I had the ball at my toe, and I was just about to make a perfect cross, the sort that makes the

crowd gasp, when wham!
top of me, and the ball's g
Do you know what Patel sh
me? "Get stuck in!" he said. The
was, doing my utmost, placed by him
in completely the wrong position,
unable to show my true skills, and all
he could do was criticise.

No wonder I got cramp. At least it could have been the start of cramp. There was a definite feeling of something about to seize up. I knew it could come on any minute.

No one can say I didn't go out bravely. There was a throw-in, and their big forward came running out, punting the ball along in front of him. Talk about getting stuck in! I went for the ball like a tiger, but then thought my cramp might be coming on, so I gave a cry, started to hobble, then fell right in the mud, holding my leg. It was a beautiful fall, as good as any I've ever seen on TV.

"Aaah, cramp!" I gasped. "Just when I was about to get the ball. It's no good. I'll have to go off. Blast it."

"Sure, Charlie," said Patel, as if he couldn't care less. No thanks, no

sympathy. His star player cut down
through no fault of my own, and he
couldn't give a hoot. I did a specially
big limp coming off the field, just to let
him know. I went to the pavilion to
rest and get some of Abdullah's
half-time grub. I wish I hadn't stayed.
Talk about being sick as a parrot.

5. The Mother
(Mrs Carrie Sandford)

HONESTLY, THAT REFEREE! What a fuss. I don't see why he couldn't have accepted me as a substitute. There was poor old Skimpole Street, only eight players on the field, being hopelessly beaten by Stapleton Road. All these Stapleton boys looked bigger, too. Maybe they've been adding things to their food in the school canteen, like those athletes you hear about. They're a funny lot up there at Stapleton.

Anyway, I was going to Safeways, with little Gavin in his pushchair, when I thought I'd look in at

Willoughby Park and see how Gary's football team was getting on. My Gary should be the captain, really. He'd be a very good captain. But Mr Watkins made that little Patel boy the captain, don't ask me why. You can have your guess and I'll have mine. Even when

Gary's grandpa went to all that trouble to be trainer, his own grandson couldn't be captain. Is that fair?

"What's the score, Dad?" I asked. I could see it wasn't going well. He looked as if he needed one of his purple pills to calm him down.

"Seventeen-nil," he said. "It's not a football match. It's the Battle of Waterloo."

Then that terrible little show-off

Charlie Gibson went off with cramp. At least he was saying he had cramp. There were only eight of them left. I think I decided there and then. But I waited for a while.

"Come on, Skimpole Street!" I shouted. "Come on, Gary!" It was hopeless. Even as I stood there, they scored again. I could see my Gary struggling bravely. Then I saw him being elbowed aside by a long, skinny boy when he tried to get at the ball.

"Hey, ref," I called out. "Have you got your eyes in your bottom? How much are the other side paying you?"

Fair comment, wouldn't you say? But he gave me a nasty, cold look.

"It's no good, Dad," I said. "I can't stand this. I'd sooner go on myself than watch poor Gary's side being massacred."

"You can't go on, Carrie," he says.
"Why not? I'll be a substitute."
Luckily I had my good strong
lace-up shoes on, because that field
was turning into a sea of mud.

51

"Just keep an eye on little Gavin,"
I said. "Put his dummy back in if it
drops out."

Then I was on the field. They all
looked a bit surprised.

"Come on, Skimpole Street," I
called.

My dad taught me years ago to play
football. In the end I was better than
the boys. Even they had to admit it.
And I still enjoy an occasional
kickabout with my Gary.

I got the ball off the tall, skinny boy
in no time at all. He just stood there
with his mouth open while I tackled
him. Then I went up the field with the
ball at my toe, and Skimpole Street
behind me. It was a wonderful feeling.
I could hear the referee blowing his
stupid whistle behind me somewhere.

"I'm Gibson's substitute!" I shouted
over my shoulder, and kept going. The
defence hadn't a chance. I sold them a
dummy as easy as anything, then as
the keeper started to go for his right, I
gave the ball a left-footer which sent it

neatly into the back of the net. The
Skimpole Streeters raised a cheer.
There's nothing like scoring a goal to
make you feel really satisfied.

"Well done, Mum," said Gary.

"One down, eighteen to go," I said.
"We'll beat them yet."

Then up came the referee.

"What do you think you're doing?
This is a schools football match."

"Yes, well, I'm the Skimpole Street
substitute."

"Are you a pupil?" he asks, with a

nasty sneer on his face.

"I'm on the PTA Committee. If that's not official, I don't know what is. Now, shall we kick off again?"

"Madam," says the ref, taking a deep breath, "I must ask you to leave the field. According to the rules of football, substitutes may only join the game by prior arrangement with the referee, and only while play is stopped. Improper substitutes are not permitted."

"Improper? Are you calling me
improper?"

He stood there with his arms folded.
He looked just like my little Gavin
does if you take a jam doughnut away
from him.

"Madam, either you leave the field,
or I will abandon the game without
more ado."

I could see he meant it. I didn't
know then that a dog had just bitten
his bottom, but I could see he was in a
funny state of mind. His eyes had a
wobbly look.

"I've been a referee for twenty
years," he said, "and I've never had a
day like this."

"Very well," I said, keeping my
dignity. "The referee's decision is final.
I know the rules. Is it fair? No. Is it
just? No. But keep your hair on. I can

tell when I'm not wanted. I will withdraw. But at least you could allow the goal."

"Certainly not."

"What a rotter," I muttered, as I went back to the sidelines. But the Skimpole Streeters gave me a cheer, and I waved back to them. I didn't stay, though. It was too painful to watch.

Now they've elected me to be their Chief Trainer, and we have sessions every Wednesday. If I don't turn them into the best school side in the land, my name's not Carrie Sandford. And I've started the Skimpole Street PTA Ladies' Team. We've already issued a challenge to the Stapleton Road mums. We'll make mincemeat of them! Actually, in view of what happened at half-time in the boys' match, that's a rather tasteless way to put it. Let's just say we'll trounce them.

6. The Centre-Half
(Gary Sandford)

MY DAD'S A SAILOR. He's on a nuclear submarine. I can't tell you any more, because it's top secret. Except I can say this, he's the most important man on the ship. He's not the captain, he's the cook.

"After three months under water, the only thing that keeps them sane is my Chicken Rissoles," he says. When he went off last time, he said to me:

"Gary, you're the man of the house now. Take care of your mum for me, won't you. You know what a helpless little thing she is."

Then he winked at me and jumped into the minicab with his holdall quick before my mum could get at him.

"Gary Sandford can't even take care of his own socks," she shouted, but he was already away.

"Right," said my mum. "If you're looking after me, you can start by making me a nice cup of tea."

"You've just had one, with Dad," I said.

"Well, I want another one."

She's always a bit sniffly after my dad goes off on one of his tours of duty. I went into the kitchen with Gavin to put the kettle on again, and I heard her talking to herself in the sitting-room.

"Pull yourself together, Carrie Sandford," she was saying. "Don't be a snibbling driveller."

That's one of our jokes. Any time little Gavin cries, she says to him: "Don't be a dribbling sniveller. Or do I mean a snivelling dribbler? Or a snibbling driveller?"

What's all this got to do with that

62

terrible football match? Well, my mum
never drank the tea I made. She came
bursting through into the kitchen and
said:

"Come on, you landlubbers, outside!
We'll have a kickabout, to take our
mind off things."

No one else's mum plays football with them. My mum doesn't care what anyone thinks, though. She spends hours taking penalty kicks or trying out different tackles. So I wasn't really surprised to see her coming on to the field.

There were only two good things about that match. One was my mum coming on and scoring a goal. I know she wasn't supposed to, but she was terrific. The whole side cheered her when she went off.

The other good thing was the ride in the ambulance. I've always wanted to be in an ambulance that goes racing along with its blue lights flashing and its siren going wee-ooo, wee-ooo, wee-ooo, and all the traffic pulling out of its way to let it through. The only trouble was that I was feeling too bad

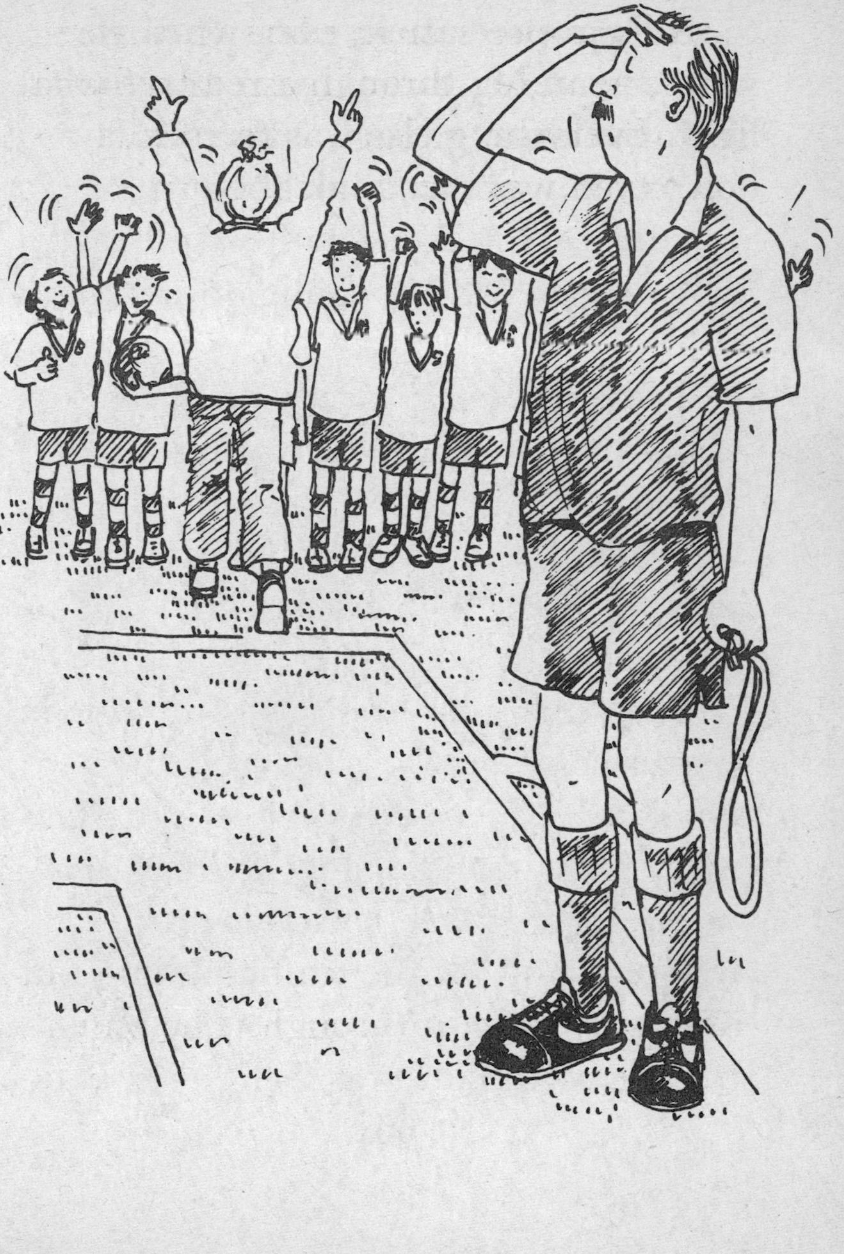

to really appreciate it, even when we went screaming through a red traffic light. Everything else was terrible. I don't even want to think about it.

7. *The Second Defender (Norman Brown)*

I DON'T KNOW what Kevin said, but whatever it was, don't believe it. He's a rotten little liar.

Of course, I was just trying to help him out a bit. He's not as fast as me, because he's too lazy to train properly, so I thought I should cover a bit more of the ground. Also, not that I'm boasting, I've got more talent than he has.

Was he grateful? He's never grateful. Instead of saying thank you, he hits me. Well, I wasn't going to take that from him. I'll tell you something about

Kevin. He still sleeps with his thumb in his mouth. He's a bit of a baby, really. He always waits to see what I do, then he does it too, or wants to.

He's jealous, of course, just because I'm the older twin. Our mum says she wishes she'd never told us who came first. But I can't help being first, can I? That entitles me to say he's my little brother, doesn't it?

I knew Kevin was in a bad mood, that day. He was moaning about his sore ear. He's always got an ache or a pain somewhere. He's not a healthy type like me. Then he complained at breakfast because I took three Weetabix and only left two for him. Well, I was there first. He would have done the same to me.

He'd been in a sulk ever since, pretending to be still hungry, even

though he had four big slices of toast
and peanut butter. I saw him looking
into his peanut butter jar and making
a face. Anyone else wouldn't notice
that some of it had gone, but greedy
old Kevin notices everything to do
with food.

Luckily, he doesn't know it was me
that took some. I only borrowed a little
bit. Well, a fairly little bit. I say I like

the crunchy sort better, but I don't
really. But Kevin said he liked smooth
peanut butter, and if I'd said, "I do
too," he'd say, "Copy cat, copy cat, go
and eat a mouldy rat." Anyway, I
don't want to like the same sort of
peanut butter as Kevin.

I don't like to put the blame on
others, but it was all Kevin's fault the
samosas got spilled. When Mr Watkins
told us to pick up the trays, I knew he
was going to do something. He was
going to give me a kick or a shove, I
could just tell. So I gave him a push,
sort of, quite a gentle one. Just to let
him know not to try anything clever.
But he's so clumsy. His tray tipped
over, then he fell against me and made
me drop my tray, and all the samosas
went in a heap. Then he had the nerve
to say it was my fault! I would have

given him a good thumping, if
Windbag Watkins wasn't standing
right over us.

That's something else about Kevin. He always has to put the blame on someone else. It's never his fault. Oh, no, good little Kevin never does anything wrong. And he gets away with everything. It had to be me that ate one of the wrong samosas, not him. And then he said it served me right! I'm going to put worms in his bed.

8. The Headmaster
(Mr Gareth Watkins)

IN MY VIEW, Skimpole Street did jolly
well, jolly well. Yes, we lost. Yes, we
were disqualified from the competition.
Yes, the game had to be abandoned
after the unpleasant scenes at
half-time. Yes, the police interviewed
Mr Abdullah of the Genghis Khan
Fast Food Takeaway. But in the end
nothing could be definitely proved, and
there were no charges. And young
Patel and his team tried really hard.
Most of them did, anyway.

However big the disaster, always
Think Positive, that's what I always do

73

myself, and that's the advice I give my pupils, too. Look at the plus side. We have our fine new football kit for when we're allowed to rejoin the inter-schools football league. And the lads have learned a lot from their defeat. With Mrs Sandford now as Chief Trainer, they are becoming a really strong side. Young Bayram Abdullah has got very keen on football, and is beginning to look, well, if not exactly slim, certainly less stout than before.

I know that Mr Abdullah meant well. It was kind of him to offer to supply half-time refreshments. When I was a boy in the Welsh Valleys we were lucky to get half an orange to suck at half-time.

"This is a feast, a perfect feast, Mr Abdullah," I said, when he arrived

with his little van and started to
unload trays of food. In fact, I had to
ask him to leave most of it aside, for
after the match. It's not good to eat too
much right in the middle of the game.
But Mr Abdullah was particularly
keen that they should at least sample
the samosas.

"I've prepared two lots, Mr Watkins. One for Skimpole Street, that's this tray here, and that one for the enemy."

"The enemy, Mr Abdullah? It's only a game, you know."

"I was watching that first half, Mr Watkins," he said. "Until I had to go and collect the food. They were murdering our poor boys. But we'll see what happens in the second half."

He had a curious gleam in his eye,

but I thought nothing of it at the time.

Mr Abdullah went to fetch some drinks from his van, and I saw the Brown twins standing about idly. That's something I can't abide.

"Come on, you two. Do something useful. Kevin, take this tray to the Stapleton Road side. Norman, pass this one around our own lot. Carefully, now."

Did Norman bump Kevin, or did Kevin bump Norman? It's always hard to tell with the Brown twins. Anyway, no sooner had these two boys picked up their trays than they seemed to collide, and the samosas all fell in a heap on the floor. Kevin glared at Norman. Norman glared at Kevin.

"You pushed me."

"Please sir, he pushed me."

"Never mind, never mind, pick them up. Quickly, now. Wretched boys."

Luckily it was a clean part of the floor, and the pastries looked none the worse for their little accident. Kevin stomped off to the Stapleton Road side with his tray. I sampled one of the samosas myself. It was deliciously warm and spicy.

"Jolly good," I said to Mr Abdullah, who had come back in with a carton of rather unsuitable fizzy drink cans.

"You've done us proud, Mr Abdullah, proud, what with the new strip and these excellent refreshments as well."

"It was nothing," said Mr Abdullah, politely. "Did the enem— the other team get their samosas?"

"Indeed they did," I told him. "The two lots got a bit mixed up, as it

78

happens, but of course that doesn't matter a bit."

"Oh, no!" cried Mr Abdullah, looking suddenly horrified. He turned to the boys.

"Don't eat them! Don't touch those samosas."

Even as he spoke, young Vernon
Cramb uttered a wail, clutched his
stomach, and dashed out of the room.
The tray of samosas was almost empty.
Eleven hungry boys don't take long to
clear the decks.

Gary Sandford gave a low moan and
followed Cramb out of the room at
high speed. Mr Abdullah turned to
me, his eyes filled with dismay.

"This has all gone terribly wrong!"
he cried.

"What do you mean?"

"They should not have been mixed up. Our boys should not have eaten the other team's samosas."

"But why ever not?"

"I put a little something into them, Mr Watkins. Quite harmless, really. Just to give our boys a chance, you see . . . "

Unfortunately, I could not wait to hear the rest of his explanation.

Something very strange was happening inside me. It was as if several angry hedgehogs had started fighting in my stomach. I had to make a run for the door, pushing past Mr Davis, the referee, who was looking green and shouting something about being poisoned.

Willoughby Park's pavilion does not boast a telephone, but old Mr Hitchin

saw it was an emergency, whizzed off in his wheelchair, and rang for an ambulance.

Needless to say, the game was abandoned. Apart from myself and the referee, five of our side and six from Stapleton Road were affected by the doctored samosas. The effect very soon wore off, and they didn't keep us in hospital. Once they'd pumped our stomachs out, they said we could go home.

But Mr Davis the referee was bitter, very bitter.

"I shall be making a full report of everything," he said to me. "If I do nothing else before I give up being a referee for ever, I shall make sure that your school is banned from the inter-school league for a very long time."

"Come now, Mr Davis," I said. "Let's Think Positive about this. I'm sure there are extenuating circumstances."

"Extenuating poppycock!" he snapped. "I have been kicked by a boy, attacked by a dog, insulted by a woman, and finally poisoned. Perhaps you'd like to set my hair on fire, or hit me on the head with a hammer, just to round things off."

"Now, now. You're not yourself. You'll feel better tomorrow, I'm sure."

"If I survive until then," he said, coldly. "Goodbye. You will hear from my solicitors."

Some people just can't see the Positive Side, can they?

Now I always say that no experience is so bad that you can't draw something positive from it. And it

84

happened again this time. It was
actually young Ashton Jackson who
gave me the idea. Fortunately he had
eaten nothing at half-time, or I would
never have heard the end of it from
Mrs Jackson.

"What have you learned from the
match, Ashton?" I asked the lad.

"I think I'll stick to tiddlywinks

in future," he replied.

As I gazed at the boy, the Positive Thought leapt into my mind.

"Tiddlywinks? Hmm, that's an interesting idea. Indoor game, requires little equipment, good for developing hand-and-eye co-ordination. Excellent. We'll start a school tiddlywinks league.

Who knows, it may become a craze
and sweep the country. And it will all
have started at Skimpole Street School.
We'll have television crews round,
newspapers . . . "

I thought I heard young Jackson
murmur, "Oh, no." But I may have
been mistaken.

9. *The Inside Right (Bayram Abdullah)*

FOOTBALL IS TOPS! I love it. I always wanted to play, but they always said I was too fat. I only got picked for the game with Stapleton Road because my dad donated the strip. Patel told me.

"Just try and keep out of the way," he said. "If the ball comes to you, kick it to one of us. If you can."

But I was the one who nearly created a goal for us. And he missed the penalty kick. He scored a beaut on someone's greenhouse, though. I thought the match was great. Even though it was only half a game, and it rained nearly all the time, and we were beaten twenty-two nothing, and got covered in mud, it was still good fun. It's nice to be part of a team. And next time, I want to take the penalty.

I won't miss.

Also in Young Puffin

SEE YOU AT THE MATCH

Margaret Joy

"It's a goal!"

The six stories in this collection are all about young football fans who watch or play the game that makes them so happy...or sad! Experience with them the excitement of your first match and the thrill of scoring the winning goal, as well as the disappointment when your team loses or you miss the big match.